JOAN

JOAN

PAUL YOUNG

To the seven million women who worked in so many
ways to support the British war effort.

"Never in the field of human conflict was so much owed by so many to so few."

—Sir Winston Churchill

Chapter one

Over-sexed, overpaid and over here

Protecting the tops of their heads with their hands, the nurses screamed as they raced through the draughty, darkened hospital corridors. None of them knew if they were laughing with fun or with fear, the joy of a shared experience or the grim knowledge that bats were flying just inches above their heads.

Joan kept up with the others, excited and squealing and screeching at the thought of these flying creatures 'preparing to land' on top of them, or feeling their claws in her neatly-combed hair.

She couldn't believe how much her life had changed. One moment she was living at home with her mum, dad, brother and the twins, working as a bookkeeper at the local Co-op. Life as she'd always known it in peacetime. Now here she was, one of a committed group of nurses, playing a vital part in Allied efforts to win the war. She felt proud. A foot taller.

On the other hand, she had witnessed injuries she could never have imagined in her earlier days. She'd seen airmen traumatised and devastated, sometimes unable to talk, often knowing their time on this earth was coming to an end. She was in no doubt about how important her role was. As well as assisting the doctors, administering injections and checking on her patients, she was a dispenser of kindness, compassion and care. What more did these fine men need than the help she and her colleagues could give at the most vulnerable time of their lives? She may not have been on what most people thought of as the front line of battle, but she was on her own front line: soothing the devastated, calming the frightened, dedicating herself to everyone on her ward, those who could be healed and the many who tragically could not.

Joan was based at the hospital near the US Air Force base named RAF Stansted Mountfitchet. The base had been opened in August 1943 and become home to the 344th Bombardment Group in February 1944, with its twin-engine B-26 Marauders. They were preparing for Operation Overlord, the codename for the Battle of Normandy, that was to launch the successful invasion of Nazi-occupied Western Europe. Six hundred aircraft from the 344th also flew over the beaches of France to attack the enemy on D-Day. Joan was working to support these ranks of true heroes.

The airfield was a maintenance and supply depot used by the RAF – everyone's aircraft needed to be in the best of shape – but most of Joan's patients were US airmen: pilots, co-pilots and the rest of the crew from the B-26 bombers. They left the airfield at Stansted, in the northeast of London, to rain their bombs on enemy targets, day and night. Other patients were civilians, victims of the Blitz whose homes had been destroyed and who'd been brought to the wards shocked, injured – sometimes critically – and in need of expert care.

Everyday she'd hear the almost deafening rumble of American planes leaving for Germany in their groups of two and three. Joan, focused on her work, had promised herself she wouldn't fall for any of these handsome pilots swilling around the air force base near Bishop's Stortford.

'Over-sexed, overpaid and over here' is what everyone said about them. They were generous with their chocolate rations and their nylons, and this impressed some of the other nurses. Many of them – more than she could count if she'd stopped to think about it – had flashed their film-star smiles when Joan walked past.

'Just one side of the story,' thought Joan. Time and again she'd witnessed the grim way these transatlantic love stories could end. She watched every night as the queues of young men, so many still in their late teens and early twenties, filed towards their aircraft ready to play their part in the war against Hitler. She watched them go with fear in her heart and a knot in her stomach. She learnt every day of the many who didn't return. Maybe some had been taken prisoner? Shot when they were found? Crashed and killed on landing? Who knew.

Joan tried to stop herself musing in this way, about what she didn't know. The hospital wards where she worked were filled with those casualties who had returned, some with burns covering their bodies; some whose limbs had to be removed; many whose eyesight had gone forever; others facing the distress and agony caused by shrapnel wounds. The reality of war she witnessed every working day was enough to deal with.

When Joan's patients had the energy and the will to talk, these were some of her favourite times. She loved the stories they told and learnt about their homeland and their families.

A world away even from the life she was living now! She even picked up some of their banter.

Matron was less than impressed.

"Will you do some injections for me, Nurse Dow?" she asked Joan one day.

"Okey dokey!" replied Joan, a big smile covering her face.

"We don't have 'okey dokeys' here," the matron scolded her. "I think you meant to say, 'Yes, Matron'."

"Okey dokey!" replied Joan, enthusiastic as ever.

Matron decided against reprimanding her young charge. Joan's winning personality and the care with which she carried out her duties made her a valuable member of the team. She would learn in time.

Falling for one of these American pilots was just too big a risk. Of this Joan was sure. Yet sometimes you couldn't stop things from happening. A trip to the pub in her friend's car led to a chance meeting with the most handsome man she'd laid eyes on for years. Frederick was quiet and courteous, quite the opposite to Joan herself. They shared some jokes and a laugh as they propped up the bar, followed by an introduction to John Collins cocktails and later on a cheeky kiss or three.

Joan realised Frederick was someone she could lose her head over.

She loved his practical jokes, the way he hid her drink when she went to the lavatory and claimed it had been taken while she made her way back. This was no simple crush. She felt they went well together. Maybe they had a future – and not necessarily on this side of the world. Maybe back in Philadelphia when he returned home.

Joan realised during this time with Frederick – or Freddie

as she started calling him – that she had truly never in her life been happier. She walked differently, even smiled differently. The world felt at her feet. She hoped beyond hope that he, unlike so many of his colleagues, might be spared. Love was a rare thing in this life. She watched him fly off with a hope and a prayer for his safe return, then did everything in her power to try not to think of him but focus on her vital work at hand.

To Joan, her decision to leave bookkeeping behind and become a nurse had been made a lifetime ago. This shift in her working life came from her heart as well as her head. She could think of nothing more important than supporting the war effort and now here she was, an essential part of the support needed during the D-Day landings and subsequent liberation of Europe. Millions of men and women from the US, Commonwealth and UK were contributing to the largest sea invasion of all time, playing a crucial role in bringing down Adolf Hitler and the Nazi regime.

The contribution based in southern England was enormous. Aerodromes were built, parts of Devon and Dorset were partitioned for the training of airmen, sailors and army troops. The D-Day landings had to be conducted in as efficient a way as possible. The Nazi occupation of Europe, as Churchill described in his famous 'We shall fight them on the beaches' speech, the areas in the grip of the Gestapo and the whole odious apparatus of Nazi rule, had to be sent packing. Joan couldn't have been prouder to have played her part in this, supporting those putting their lives at risk day and night, to fight for freedom and democracy, a safer land for all of their children and their children's children.

****

"Nurse Dow." Matron brought her musings to a sharp halt.

"Yes Matron," replied Joan. She was learning to use her British politeness, Matron noticed, approvingly.

"Your new patient," said Matron, crisply. "A young man badly burnt. His plane was shot down."

Joan's mind raced. Could it be Freddie? Her heartbeat rushed in her chest. Could it be true? Had he been injured? Could she help nurse him back to health?

Matron interrupted her thoughts. "His name is Hans," she said. "He is from Germany."

Chapter 2

Scott Joplin in the room

Dow Family

When Bert Dow played the piano, it was as if Scott Joplin himself was sitting in the small but comfortable living room at 49, Waverley Road in Woodford, east London. Everyone stopped talking and listened. The truth was no one could quite believe what they were hearing. They knew Bert had never been taught to read music, but miraculously the ends of his fingers delivered all the notes delicately and playfully, and all in the right order. "You 'um it and I'll play it," Bert instructed his audience and that's exactly what happened, every time.

This was Bert's little piece of joyful magic that he gifted to the world during these family sing-songs. He made everyone dance and sing and be happy; a true entertainer, just like Scott Joplin himself. His wife Lil tried to shush them when she felt their get-togethers were getting too rowdy.

"Bert, calm everyone down. What will the neighbours think? They sound like a herd of cattle," she shouted, her hands over her ears as everyone else sang along to her husband's melodies.

"Moo moo," her husband joked back. He was truly in his element.

It wasn't just the piano that Bert had mastered. He was a self-taught engineer, who could turn his hand to anything mechanical and anything to do with construction. He didn't ever need lessons or guidance; he just knew what to do. In fact, he was listed on his marriage certificate as Herbert Dow, mechanical engineer and journeyman, meaning he had a level of skill allowing him to supervise others.

As soon as war was declared, Bert started making ordnance components for shells at his engineering workshop. This wasn't an easy job. Fine engineering was needed, detailed use of the lathe. He had an inherent ingenuity and craftsmanship enabling him to work his way round any problems. That was Bert's way.

Joan adored her dad. She loved her mum, Lil, too. They were a great couple, everyone said so. But she learnt from her dad his ease on the piano keys as she watched his strong, masculine fingers find their way from chord to chord; his attention to detail at work, using as much care on everything he created as a surgeon would with a knife; his deep knowledge about the importance of doing the very best he could in whatever he was doing. She took all those lessons to heart. She buried them inside herself, and they became part of who she was too. The proud daughter of Bert Dow.

Joan watched how her dad reacted when things went wrong. He had run a garage with his friend, Gerald, just off Maybank Road where he and Lil lived in east London. In those days there was precious little travelling, and motorbikes were more popular than cars. In fact, if you had a family, you bought a sidecar to put your baby in! Motoring was starting to become more popular, and Lil worked at the garage part time as well, serving the fuel from new hand-cranked pumps. No one served themselves.

When someone owned a car and wanted to go for a journey, they'd take Bert with them in case he needed to fix a problem on the way. A thirty- or forty-mile trip was too much of a risk without a maintenance man by your side.

Business boomed until the London Underground extended the Central Line and put a kybosh on their plans. Their road was turned into a dead end and cars driving past were directed onto a new overpass. There was no longer any potential passing trade spotting their garage as somewhere to fill their tank or go for help. Joan saw how her father coped when he had to shut his business. She saw how cleverly he switched to find a new path and start working as an engineer at Gants Hill.

Lil came from a family of engineers too. Engineers stretched back for generations in the history of both families. They both hailed from east London, too; no one moved far from the area they knew in those days.

Her mum Lil, born Elizabeth Jane Cole, had a tough childhood. She was the eldest of four children and the only girl, living at 61, Sidley Road, Forest Gate. Their mother died tragically when Lil was just fourteen. Her father had to keep working, and Lil left school to care for her brothers.

She grew up quickly, searching for ways to replace her mother, trying to look after three grief-stricken brothers and her father while burying her own loss deep inside.

She met Bert when she was just twenty-one and he was a year older, and they married soon after in 1915, then settled in their first home, 138 Second Avenue, Manor Park.

Lil gave birth to first Ron and then Joan, whose birth was registered on 15th June 1919. Ron was a lovely brother to Joan, always looking out for his little sister. Then, seven or eight years later, to her great embarrassment as she was in her thirties, and very definitely 'unplanned', Lil gave birth to twin girls, Hazel and Daphne. "'Ow will we manage?" she asked her husband in desperation. Bert tried to reassure her. He told her he'd do a bit more work on the side, travelling with car owners again to help with motors that packed up. He was delighted to welcome the twins into their family. True, they didn't have much money, and Lil couldn't work as she had to look after her newborns, but they'd cleverly made the decision to buy the house they'd moved to at Waverley Road and he knew they'd cope.

Their house had two reception rooms and a kitchen downstairs, and a staircase up to three bedrooms above. The bathroom and the toilet were out in the back garden in a big, cold lean-to. The girls top-and-toed in one bedroom, Ron took another, while Lil and Bert shared the other.

Joan looked back on her childhood with love. Theirs was a

happy, happy household. Bert was a practical joker and would regale them with the most amazing stories. He came home late from work one day and told Lil one tale of woe.

"I've 'ad the most terrible time," he told his flustered wife, as she handed him his dinner, ruined by the wait. Between mouthfuls he explained. "I just went to Woolworths to get some cigarette papers," he said, just slightly indignantly. Everyone smoked in those days. Even doctors recommended it as something that calmed the nerves. Then as he went to walk out of the store, past all the ladies serving behind the counters, the manager stopped him in his tracks, placing his hand roughly on his shoulder.

"He said to me, 'I'm afraid I have to detain you. You've taken something without paying for it.'" Bert went on, "I told him I hadn't. I said, 'You've got the wrong man, mate,' But he didn't believe me. He marched me into the office at the back of the shop, passing all these ladies as I went who were all staring at me."

The office in Woolies was really just a wooden partition in the corner of the store. It wasn't even a separate room as it had an opening at its top, with a small window for the manager and staff to peer outside.

"I found myself there, in this space I'd never seen before," said Bert. "And the manager said, 'I'm going to get the police now.' He shut the door on the partition with me inside. I thought, I can't stand for this," said Bert. "So I started climbing my way out over the partition."

Lil was horrified. How could he! "The police could still be searching for you now," she told him.

She couldn't believe her husband had done such a stupid

thing. "They'll think you're guilty. You should never have done that, Bert."

Bert saw he had to explain himself. He was in trouble with his wife as well as everyone else and carried on his sorry tale. "Well, the manager came back into the office and saw me trying to escape. I had one leg over the partition and the other I was trying to pull through and over when the manager comes back and grabs me and pulls on my leg …"

The children sat round, their mouths gaping open.

Bert stopped short and paused. "… Just like I'm pulling yours now!"

What could Lil say? Yet again she'd been bamboozled by her husband's clever ways. She didn't know whether to be relieved or angry. She'd believed every word until the last moment.

She grabbed a saucepan and chased him around the room while the children sitting round the kitchen table were laughing so hard at the sight of their parents' wild goose chase, they struggled to breathe.

There were other good times. Sometimes they travelled on the 'steamer', the steam train to Southend for a day trip by the sea. Joan also spent a lot of time looking after the twins. She adored them. They played hopscotch together and skipped with old pieces of rope. At one stage, Bert managed to lay his hands on an old Monopoly set which was like nothing any of them had ever seen before.

When she had time to be alone, Joan loved reading. She devoured Shakespeare. She loved writing too. At a different time, a different future might have been planned for her, maybe in further education. As it was, school tried to encourage her and found her a penfriend, Eva, who lived in Munich, southern Germany. They wrote to each other every week, to describe their lives and interests. They loved learning about each other's families and hometowns.

All of a sudden, in the early 1930s, Eva told Joan that letters from England were no longer coming through to her. She wrote, "I'm not getting your letters. It's been several weeks now. Papa says that they might be getting stopped. It's political, he thinks."

Joan was shocked. She felt suddenly cold all over. This was a foreboding about events to come. Times might be changing in a dangerous and harsh way. There had been whispers of someone called Hitler who had risen to power and talk of a future war. Even though Joan was young, unlike others her age and thanks to Eva, she had an insight into the life of an ordinary German family. She knew all Germans weren't the enemy. She didn't want Eva's family to suffer any more than she wanted her own to. What was the world coming to?

She distracted herself from these thoughts with her day-to-day duties. There were the twins to care for, of course. Just as Lil had grown up looking after her little brothers, Joan had been taught to do the same with the little ones. On top of that she had to help with the housework: scrubbing the clothes with a washboard; pushing them through the ringer and turning and turning the handle to squeeze as much water out from them as she could; then hanging up the clean washing. They had a clothes airer on a pulley attached to the kitchen ceiling. Sometimes they'd all sit down to eat, and one of them would get a drop of water on their plate, to howls of laughter.

Hazel was indignant on one occasion, seeing the splatters

on her dinner. "That's your thick jumpers, Joan," she complained.

"It's not," countered Joan. "Anyhow, I'm not wringing it – it'll go out of shape."

Sometimes Joan helped prepare food for the family. Theirs was a traditional diet, not much chicken in those days, but plenty of pork and occasionally beef on a Sunday. They made gravy from the juice of the meat and the water from the vegetables.

Joan's older brother Ron didn't join in with the domestic work – well, he was a boy – but like his father he was useful around the house. He was a joker like his dad and great company for all of them. As he grew older, after he left home, he'd come back and enjoy a beer or two with Bert while Lil sipped a gin.

In general, though, there was equality in the house. In many homes, girls were not expected to progress in any way. Their job was to help in the home, find a husband, and look after their own home, while the men worked. This was not the case at the Dows, where they knew Joan could get herself a good job and do well in her life.

Joan loved animals. Her Uncle Alec, Lil's brother, was in the Merchant Navy, and his ship had visited Buenos Aires in Argentina. He brought his niece back a beautiful yellow canary. Joan spent hours poking her finger through the bars of his cage in the front room of their terraced house, watching him play with a tiny mirror. At times the family had a dog, but the pet Joan loved most was her rabbit, Simon. A present from her dad. She loved feeding him and cleaning out his cage and letting him run round the garden, then treating him to a bed of fresh wooden shavings.

Joan confided in her dad that she would love to be a vet when she was older. "It's animals," she said to him. "I love them and I think they love me too."

This slightly broke Bert's heart. He knew they weren't from the social class that would get his lovely daughter that kind of education.

He would have loved her to follow her dream. He gave her his biggest smile. "You'll find something you're great at," he told her. "I promise you that."

Chapter 3

War takes over

When war was declared in September 1939, few could have realised the impact this would have across the country. Everybody's life changed.

In the Dow household, Bert's work shifted to creating munitions to support the war effort. Ron joined the army. The girls did all they could to keep their lives feeling normal, but everyone knew what was happening in the wider world. Every family huddled round a valve radio, listening to the Light Programme. The radio was a large, veneered box with a central knob for tuning. The dial was lit by a green light that changed intensity when a station was found. Bert and Ron were best at finding the stations. The BBC ran the Light Programme and the Home Programme. If you were really skilled, you could manage to use shortwave to find the World Programme. Every family member would wait patiently for the voice being transmitted that informed them of the latest developments, to learn about casualties and pray that better days were ahead.

Gradually they were affected in other ways. Food rationing became more and more extensive. Sugar, coffee, fats, fish, cheese and meat were restricted for every household across the country.

Suddenly there were uniforms everywhere. Ron came back into the house in his REME uniform – he had joined the Royal Electrical and Mechanical Engineers. He was off to train at Basingstoke. Joan felt a tear coming when he walked back out of the front door. She knew the Nazis had marched into Austria, then Czechoslovakia. The Prime Minister Neville Chamberlain had met with Adolf Hitler and agreed a treaty that Hitler had promptly broken by marching into Poland, Britain's allies. Europe was thrown into war.

"That pesky rabbit is eating too much," thought Lil, when she went out to give some scraps to Joan's special pet. This worried her deeply. She knew how much Joan loved her rabbit, but the family had to come first. She watched as lettuce and carrots disappeared in front of her eyes. "We're not given ration books for a rabbit," Lil grumbled. She was working hard to stretch the family's food allowance to cover them all. The rabbit was a mouth to feed that she didn't need.

That evening Lil said she wasn't hungry when she served the family some meat stew.

Everyone was concerned for her.

"Leave me be. Stop fussing," she scolded them.

Reluctantly they turned their attention to their dinner. It certainly smelt good.

"Is it chicken?" asked Bert. "You've done a grand job here, Lil."

The others tucked in.

"I'm a bit under the weather," Lil told them. "Don't you worry about me. I'm not so 'ungry. You help yourselves."

Joan thought this was strange. Until now they'd only had some scraps of pork belly to last the week. She did as she was told and happily scraped her plate clean – that's what everyone did, every day. Then she strolled outside to take a couple of carrot tops to her pet. Her walk soon turned into a run and then a race to the end. She twigged what had happened before she saw the empty cage. Her mum had killed, skinned and chopped up her little rabbit, her friend. That was what they'd been chewing on inside. She ran back and turned on her mother.

"I can't believe what you've done!" she shouted at her.

Lil turned white with guilt. "I had no choice, love; family has to come first," she tried to explain. A sudden thought: "Don't tell the twins. They'll be too upset," she begged her daughter. The two of them stood sobbing together. It took weeks for Joan to forgive her mum, no matter how hard she tried to understand.

By this time, Joan had left school, taken a bookkeeping course and had found work at the Co-op. She excelled at bookkeeping, in part the result of her ability to focus on detail that she'd learnt from her father. Joan enjoyed her on-the-job training, especially working with men. Women, she had decided by then, could be bitchy; men were more fun. The men loved Joan too. Her striking looks and hourglass figure meant they melted at just one smile from her. Not just at work: she'd happily flirt with the butcher who'd give her an extra sausage or slice of bacon in return when she went to collect her rations.

Lil was very worried during the air raids. She had witnessed bombing from German Zeppelins in the First World

War, close to where she lived. That kind of destruction and devastation had horrific ramifications. You couldn't know the truth of it unless you were there, she told herself. She so didn't want her children to experience the same.

Joan had strong feelings about the war too. She hated Hitler with a passion, and idolised Churchill. Everyone listened to his speeches intently. He was the true voice of the nation. Chamberlain waving his papers in the air, claiming he had won a peaceful accord with Hitler? "A waste of time." Joan almost spat these words. Churchill was the one they depended on, to a man and a woman and a child.

Joan wasn't frightened though. Not for herself. She feared for her mum and dad. She feared for her brother. Ron was in Egypt supporting the African Campaign, letters the only form of communication. She feared for the safety of her sisters, but never for herself. She knew she might get home safely from work and she might not. Life was a lottery. She was going to take what she could from it while she could. This may sound a strange way to live, but what else could you do? If the air raid was sounding, you could rush to the nearest shelter but you might not make it. In London she might find herself in an Underground station for protection, but they were living in Woodford, further out and above ground. There was an underpass at South Woodford, but this was a mile away if you walked, or five minutes on the number 10 bus. Of course, like everyone else, she carried around her gas mask wherever she went, and she always had a clean handkerchief to dab away her tears or anyone else's if this was needed, maybe someone who'd lost a brother, sister, husband, mother or father. These things happened every day, after all.

The Dow family, like all others, knew some of the casualties of war personally. In better times a host of young men, friends of Ron's, had been keen to come round for cups of tea, not least to spend time with Ron's attractive sister Joan, listening to her playing the piano with her amusing younger sisters. The loss of any of these fine young people was a great sadness to them. A hole in their lives. Joan would notice customers at the Co-op who had stopped coming in, then widows in black with fewer ration stamps than before. Silent tragedies happening in front of them all.

Like everyone she took warning signs very seriously. When it was time for blackouts, for everyone to cover their windows to disguise the location of residential areas from German bombers, she joined the others in rushing to get this done. The whole area would turn black and anyone not doing their job well enough would hear a knock on their door from an air raid warden, often retired soldiers, sometimes officious in their demands.

The air raid wardens also checked everyone was in their air raid shelters when the sirens sounded. The shelters weren't that safe, but the only alternative was standing under a doorway at home or crouching under a table, and a shelter was better than either of those options.

The Dow family had its own Anderson shelter in the back garden in case of air raids. Bert, with Ron's help, had built it himself: a corrugated roof over concrete foundations, with sandbags inside, covered with earth for added protection against bomb blasts.

The shelter was cold and uncomfortable, and a squeeze for the whole family to fit in, but they felt safer in it than at home. Daphne suffered most in the damp cold as she was the weaker of the two. Joan always thought the cold and damp may have contributed to her later being diagnosed with TB, though she had good care in Switzerland after the war and recovered. There was no need to make room for Ron in their hidey-hole. He'd received his call-up papers and was training in a makeshift army barracks in Ongar. Soon afterwards he was posted to Egypt to join Montgomery to fight the war in North Africa.

Often the Dows had to spend all night in the shelter, listening to the bombing in the centre of London, far enough away for them not to worry about their immediate safety. They shivered, nonetheless. All they had for warmth was a blanket and a hot water bottle that soon cooled.

"Cuddle up Joan," said ten-year-old Hazel, always the more outspoken one of the twins. Joan was pleased to hug them as hard as she could to keep them warm. She loved them to bits and no mistake. An old oil lamp gave them a flicker of light and a little bit of comfort, and she brushed their hair gently with her fingers and kissed the tops of their foreheads.

The shelters weren't always used as protection against the bombs themselves. More often, they stopped people being trapped or killed by the aftermath, the falling rubble and masonry. The earth and sandbags gave some protection against flying pieces of red-hot metal: shrapnel caused by the shattering of the metal casing around the bombs when the explosive inside was detonated.

On one September night in 1943, the air raid siren sounded around teatime. The sound of the bombs seemed to be closer than they'd heard before, shaking their very bones.

They all knew the German bombers made a droning noise; the RAF fighters had a higher pitch.

The family listened out to hear what was happening. Had we managed to shoot down any of their planes? One seemed to hit the ground some miles away and the twins cheered with excitement.

Not Lil. She knew the reality, the tragedy, the destruction.

To their relief, Woodford had remained unscathed.

Joan feared for her family, for the home they knew so well, the community where they knew every step of pavement, every turn in the street, every front door, every weed that grew in the cracks of the road. The droning became louder and louder. The air raid sirens filled the air. Then the bombs fell, first with an eerie whistle, giving a sign that life might be about to change forever, then a shatteringly loud crack and crash. A succession of explosions getting closer and closer, the ground shaking with each explosion. Joan had never heard anything like the mighty sound of the sticks of bombs falling around ten at a time.

The bombs started hitting Woodford soon afterwards. The Dows squeezed each other's hands as tight as they could. This was really happening to them. They heard bombs landing in fields with a thud, missing their targets, then loud explosions closer to their shelter. They could taste the dust and the chloride in the air. Joan tried to keep calm while tears silently ran down her face. She had to protect the twins.

Worse followed. An explosion so close it shook them to their bones, their ears stinging with the sound. Straight away came the noise of masonry and timber crashing to the ground. It was like crouching in the middle of an earthquake.

"Was the house hit?" whispered Hazel.

Bert admitted he didn't know.

Lil could no longer hide her nerves. "I need a fag," the rest of them heard her say, her voice a faint rasp.

Why bomb Woodford? This was surely a mistake. The Germans must have flown off course, mistaking the bend in the local River Roding for the bend in the River Thames where the manufacturing bases of the Thames Valley produced vital bullets, bombs and shells. It certainly wasn't unusual for bombs to miss their intended target. It happened all the time.

The bombers had finished their worst, emptying the rest of their bombs onto fields some way away, and flying back to refill. Sirens were now sounding, giving the all-clear. The family emerged shocked and blinking from their hiding hole.

Usually their first stop was the race for their outside loo as they stepped into the real world. Instead they rushed to the front of their home to see the damage that had been done.

A bomb had landed squarely on the two houses opposite the Dow's in Waverley Road. The neighbours' houses had been destroyed. Of that there was no question.

Their own was badly damaged, the roof crushed and not a window left in its place. Unbelievable. This was their happy place, full of piano music and the worst practical jokes you could imagine. Now they crunched glass underfoot as they went from room to room wondering what their futures held.

"Look at that!" shrieked Joan. The back wall of their front room was covered with spikes of deadly glass embedded like shrapnel, but Joan wasn't looking at the wall at all. Her mouth dropped open. It was a miracle.

In the midst of this carnage sang the bright yellow canary,

the present from Uncle Alec, still chirping away. Every single piece of glass had missed him. It was like a knife thrower had thrown a thousand tiny sharp weapons all around the little bird, each one missing him and sticking into the wallpaper round his cage. There he sat and not a feather missing. Perfectly healthy and happy.

The Germans couldn't destroy everything!

Chapter 4

Homeless

The air raid warden tut-tut-tutted as he walked around the ruins of the front of their house.

"Structural damage," he wrote in his notebook with his scratchy pencil. He took Bert to one side and told him his verdict. He was concerned the whole house might collapse. They needed to leave.

Lil and the girls were in tears, consoling each other. Their home, their life, had been destroyed in seconds. Joan couldn't stop crying as they clung to each other, standing in the street. Neighbours were out inspecting the damage; there was rubble in every direction.

Number 20 and 22 opposite had had a direct hit from a 500lb bomb that had almost totally demolished the pair of them. Personal belongings from the Graves's and Jones's who had lived there were strewn around the street. Joan saw a pretty, delicate teacup with its ornate handle sticking out of the rubble.

"Look!" Joan walked over and picked it up. "It's unmarked," she said, blowing off the dust.

Luckily everyone had been in the shelters, so quite

miraculously no one had been injured.

Bert, Lil and the three girls packed the stuff they could take with them, and gave the canary to one of the neighbours, Janice.

"Poor little thing," she told them. "I'll look after it for you."

Then they were guided away from their wrecked home by the local air raid warden, David Elliot, a retired ex-army soldier who'd seen service in the First World War. He was so helpful. Like the family, he was surprised by the bombing in Woodford.

"Probably a stray plane, just wanting to drop his bombs and go home," he said. "We'll have to make the house secure. There's been some looting in east London," he told them.

"It's devastating," Lil remarked. "We're just civilians."

Bert put his arm around her as they walked away.

They soon realised the electricity, gas and water supplies in the neighbourhood had been destroyed. Fires rose around them as escaping gas met discarded cigarette ends and flared in the streets.

Their destination was Holy Trinity Church Hall in Maybank Road, just half a mile away.

'It's funny the way everything changes when you think things will stay the same forever,' thought Joan, as they made their way through the familiar streets, now covered in rubble, taking care not to stumble over the bricks and debris.

On arriving at the hall, they found they were not the only family who were officially homeless. Fifteen other families were sharing the space. They gave their names and addresses to a volunteer and, in return, were given blankets and each told to claim a put-up bed.

They lay there with little to do while they waited for details about what would happen to them next. Lil tried to distract the girls, making jokes about the elastic in their knickers.

"It's getting so loose they'll be falling round our ankles," she laughed, and managed to wangle some needles and cotton and persuaded the girls to tighten up their drawers. At least it was something to do.

They whispered comments to each other about their new circumstances and who else they were sharing their space with. All agreed that the worst thing about the hall was the queue for the toilet.

"Make sure you do it all," Lil kept hissing at the girls when they finally reached their turn, as if they were five years old. "We ain't got time to queue again."

It was while they were standing in this blasted queue, that Joan was handed a letter. Her eyes opened wide, in shock and delight in equal measure.

"I know who this is from," she told no one and everyone standing around her. She saw the NAAFI postmark. They'd all been waiting for ages to get word from him. It was Ron!

Chapter 5

A card from Ron

Ron Dow was stationed in Cairo, Egypt, part of the Royal Electrical and Mechanical Engineers in the consignment of British and Commonwealth troops protecting the Suez Canal and Britain's oil supplies. Their eyes widened as she read out his news – Ron had been promoted to corporal for doing a bit of rail work!

Ron was typical of servicemen in that he never really took credit for his brave actions. In fact, he never disclosed the full story to his family for fear of causing any anxiety at home.

Ron was nothing but modest about that day when he'd been standing on the platform at Cairo's main railway station with around two hundred and fifty other troops on the platforms, some waiting for transport, others unloading the wagons on a stationary goods train full of ammunition and other ordinance. The Germans weren't far away, shelling everything they could, and the station was a particular target. Suddenly one of the German shells hit a rear wagon of the goods train and it caught fire.

Imagine the scene and the fear that was unfolding. If the fire had spread to any of the other wagons, a disaster was heading their way, with explosions and bullets flying in all directions the result.

Ron Dow

Captain Adams immediately summoned the radio operator. "Corporal Jones!" he barked.

"Yes Sir," was the reply.

"Call for a fire truck. We have an ammunition train on fire."

"Yes Sir, immediately," Jones responded, a sign of panic in his voice as the urgency of the situation unfolded.

As the flames grew there was a popping sound as some of the ammunition went off. Thanks to steel-cased ammunition canisters, the bullets were currently being contained.

By now there was a scrabble to unload as quickly as possible, moving the steel cases of ammunition off the platform into the safety of the main building. Troops began to file down the platform away from the burning wagon. By now they could feel the heat on their faces as the flames began to roar. The popping sound had increased and loud bangs were pounding their ears. Sparks flew through the gaps in the timber walls of the wagon.

Ron and his colleges approached Captain Jones.

"Sir," Ron called, trying to attract the attention of his commanding officer.

"Dow," came the reply.

"Sir, I could uncouple the wagon with some help and stop the fire spreading to other wagons," said Ron, urgency in his voice.

Captain Jones considered the offer briefly. "You know how to uncouple it?"

"Yes, Sir." Ron paused as they all shuffled back as another shell landed nearby, hitting a tool shed. "I worked as a guard on the London Underground," explained Ron. "They taught me how to uncouple coaches, Sir."

"Is it the same, Dow?"

"Yes, Sir"

"What do you need?"

"A dozen chaps, Sir."

"Get to it," barked Captain Jones. "You chaps follow Dow's instruction. Get to it sharpish before things get out of control."

With the flames getting close to the end of the wagon, time was running out. Ron knew he had one chance at releasing the pin and uncoupling the wagon.

They all jumped down onto the track, Ron, climbing under the coupling to release the locking pin, ordered, "Take the tension off" as the guys pulled the wagon in. Thankfully the pin came out easily, it was well-greased.

"Now push hard!" Ron shouted. The coupling came apart and the wagon was free.

The heat was now getting intense but they all kept pushing until they were twenty yards down the track. Coughing from the smoke inhalation and blackened with grease and soot, Ron and the others climbed back onto the platform unscathed as the wagon continued to burn.

Now nearly completely engulfed in flames, it resembled a firework display, banging, sparking with whizzing bullets in the air as the steel canisters buckled under the heat, exposing the live ammo inside.

Joan never thought that Ron would ever be in danger as he wasn't on the front line. Her first thought on seeing the card was, 'As long as he's safe.' Little did she know what her brother had been through and everything he had achieved.

Meanwhile, Ron knew all about danger. When the African Campaign started they were sheltering behind a truck from some small arms fire. One of his colleagues decided to take a look to see where the firing was coming from as it was obvious they were not the target. Climbing on the cab, he suddenly fell to the ground with a thud.

"George, are you OK?" Ron shouted. There was no response, he'd been hit by a stray bullet, the round had taken the back of his head off.

Ron and his colleagues staggered back in shock at what they'd seen.

Ron knew this and everyone alongside him knew it too. In Cairo, the whole train, the whole station, could have gone up in flames with Ron right at the centre. He had taken a huge risk but it had worked. He had saved everyone around him and was mentioned in despatches by his superior officer in his report to the War Office for his bravery, leadership and skill.

Chapter 6

The journey

The family wasn't at the church hall for long. Some days later they heard from the billeting officer that, to their surprise, they were heading to Scotland. Well, most of them.

The twins, who by now were fourteen, were being evacuated to Lugar, a village close to Kilmarnock, a small town between Glasgow and Ayr, and Lil and Joan were to go with them. Most children were evacuated to Devon or Cornwall, some sent as far afield as Canada.

Scotland hadn't been what they expected. Lil had told the powers that be that she didn't want to be separated from any of her children because she'd lost her mother when she was a teenager and couldn't bear to lose anyone else. Bert had to stay behind as he was part of the war effort, making munitions for the British army, and was billeted in lodgings near his factory.

Joan had to leave her job as a bookkeeper with the Co-op. She'd loved it there and thought wistfully of what she was leaving behind. All the younger men had been called up to join the armed forces, so those left in the office were either near retirement or disabled. She had been particularly fond of a good-looking young chap, tall and blond-haired. Jonathan had been in the Dunkirk evacuation and lost his arm because of the bombings on the beach. He was fond of her too, teasing her with comments when she, with her shapely figure, squeezed past his desk.

"You nearly knocked my eye out," he'd say to her.

"Cheeky sod," was always her reply, her favourite phrase of all time.

Scotland seemed a long way away for a family who had never before left London. Joan had never been separated from her father before either. She hated the thought, though she was a grown woman now. Her father was the person she went to for help and guidance, she trusted his instincts and his view of the world more than anyone's.

Bert got the day off to see his family go. They took the train to St Pancras Station and found it, too, had been bombed. Its glass roof had shattered though the bomb that had done the damage hadn't exploded. The twins creaked their necks, looking skywards to count the smashed panels and in awe of the magnificence of the building that remained. The noise from the crowded station took them by surprise. Central London was busy and chaotic compared to where they'd come from. They wiped their eyes as debris caused them to blink rapidly and yearn for home.

Unexploded bombs from the night before rested on the track, just fifty yards from the platforms. First bomb squads and then workmen were de-activating and clearing these, while the girls had time to play hopscotch on the platform using chalk they'd squirreled away in their pockets. An elderly gentleman, a retired captain who had been reinstalled in the army to deal with emergency situations, was not impressed.

"You can't draw here. It's a public area, not a playground," he spluttered.

The girls giggled and ran back to Lil.

Joan took her father to one side. She wanted to talk to him about something that had been on her mind. "Dad …" she began, nervously. "I was just wondering, do you think I'd make a good nurse?"

Bert considered the question carefully. "Of course you would," he replied, wholeheartedly. "You'd be a brilliant nurse. You've always been good in that way. You always wanted to be a vet, remember? You've always been good at caring for others. Look how much you've helped Mum with the twins."

Lil overheard and agreed. "You'd be a lovely nurse, Joan," she assured her.

Bert hugged all his ladies.

"Love you, Dad." "Love you, sweetheart," they chorused to and fro.

"Enjoy your journey," he told them, sounding as upbeat as he could. "Don't worry about me – and don't worry about Ron. We'll be fine."

Of course he couldn't have known that for sure and neither could they. But there was something about Bert and Ron. You felt secure in their company. Better to see them as born survivors than fear the worst.

"Bloody war, bloody Hitler," Joan said out loud. She hated leaving her dad, she could feel the tears welling in her eyes as she tried to put a brave face on it. There were tears welling in Bert eyes too. Bert pulled a handkerchief from his pocket.

Lil clutched the railway tickets that would take them on to Ayrshire. Bert asked the guard if he needed a platform ticket to wave them off, but he was ushered through. The family made their way to the platform where the sight of their train took their breath away. There were two steam locomotives on one train, and instead of eight to ten carriages there were nearer eighteen! This was a monster! It had been doubled in length to get more freight and more people moving more quickly over longer distances, using less fuel. Joan marvelled that such clever decisions were being made all the time, quietly and carefully without anyone knowing.

The platform and train were crowded. Packed. They shuffled on with their bags and gas masks, finding a spot they could call their own. There was no chance of sleeping, it was all too loud and too exciting. Bert stepped back on to the platform as the guard's whistle blew and the heavy train started to move, clanking at the couplings as the two locomotives puffed steam out of their chimneys.

Bert's eyes began to well up with tears as he waved goodbye. He pulled out his handkerchief to mop them away. Once they'd pulled away and waved goodbye to Bert, tears running down their cheeks, the family found a vacant compartment off one of the long corridors running down one side of the coach with sliding door compartments labelled with 1st, 2nd or 3rd class.

The Dow's were lucky as they had 2nd class tickets with the smart striped upholstered seats. Each coach had a toilet at each end with a notice instructing the passengers, 'Do not use in the station'. The train carriages were linked by a concertina corridor between each coach. The restaurant car was about midway, so Joan made her way along the corridors lined with servicemen puffing cigarettes out the open vent windows, above the picture windows running down each side. Joan found the restaurant carriage and had a couple of gins to calm herself. It was a bit of a squeeze as it was mostly filled with servicemen and women, hoping for a drink or snack.

The freshly made corned beef and cheese sandwiches with Branston pickle looked appealing, thought Joan, as the ladies behind the counter worked tirelessly keeping up with demand. Tea was being served from a big brown porcelain pot and poured into chipped, steel mugs with lots of sugar. Every item had been chosen to ensure it wouldn't crack if the brakes were applied too quickly and they went crashing to the floor.

The journey was slow. Sometimes the train stopped and they spent an hour or two waiting for it to start again. When it finally pulled away, the carriages would catch up with the engines and jolt everyone inside them. Besides this, the ride was steady, with the driver watching out for signal damage on the way to keep everyone safe.

Joan settled down to make the most of her adventure. The journey made her more aware of her looks than she had been before. Her curly brown hair bounced as the train chugged along. She had wondered if she would get attention from the servicemen on leave who filled most of the carriages, and she was right. As the train rattled through the countryside, she tried to remain focused on the task ahead. Relocating to a new place was stressful and she didn't need any distractions. She began the journey slightly regretting the attention she was receiving but hadn't yet passed Watford when she noticed she had begun to revel in it. It felt as if there was a soldier looking in her direction whenever she turned her head. The buttons on their crisp uniforms glistened and distracted her, making her glance from this way to that.

Everything felt exciting. She may have been on her way to a small village in Scotland but to her own mind, never having left London before, she was travelling the world. Soon the train was travelling through open countryside with woods and the odd farmyard springing into view through the constant trail of steam from the pair of steam locomotives at the front.

She took a drag of a cigarette and asked a young soldier squeezed up next to her where he was from. "Glasgae," he told her.

She introduced herself. "Joan," grabbing his hand as the train shook her nearly off her feet.

"Aye, I'm Steve." His blue eyes lit up.

"You're a long way from 'ome," remarked Joan.

"I've bin doon south, trainin' as a sniper in Basingstoke!"

"Oh," Joan replied. "What's a sniper do?"

"Aye it's important like," Steve tried to explain. "The enemy, they have snipers wi' telescopic sights. They con pick off our troops at five hundred yards."

"Oh how awful," Joan remarked.

"Aye, it is that. That's me job ta spot em en take em oot."

"It's dangerous then," said Joan, considering how much responsibility this young lad had.

"Aye, it is. And necessary too."

Joan realised how committed Steve was and to her surprise, welled up inside with emotion. "How old are you?" she asked him.

"I'm eighteen. I can't wait to get over there when the big push starts."

"Where's there? What big push?" asked Joan.

Steve put his finger to his lips. "It's all hush hush like, no one knows when or where but we're all being trained up for an amphibious landing."

Joan was full of respect for this young man. He was doing his bit, serving his country. "Good luck to you," she told him. Joan took her turn in the queue to buy a packet of ten Craven A cigarettes. "Would you like one?" she offered Steve. "You look like you could use it."

"You're right kind. Much appreciated, Joan," said the young man.

They swapped addresses. "Let me know how you get on," she told the young man.

As they smoked their cigarettes the train jolted to a halt, and they were thrown together. Joan's breasts pushed against his chest.

"I'm so sorry. I'm so sorry. I didn't mean to ... you know ..." The young soldier's voice trailed away. He couldn't decide whether he was mortified or secretly pleased at the encounter. Maybe both.

When eventually they reached Glasgow, there were more delays thanks to recent bombing.

Finally they arrived in Kilmarnock. Stepping out of their carriage, the freshness of the air startled them after all those hours cooped up inside. The Dows saw instantly how different everything was from life back in Woodford. They stared at the portcullis entrance to the station that made it look like an old fort. As they walked past it and down concrete stairs into the street below, the air still felt clearer somehow, even though they were close to collieries. Miners were exempt from military service because the coal they were digging from deep underground was the fuel vital for the nation.

Outside the station they waited in the drizzling rain at the bus stop for the bus to Lugar. Lugar was about an hour away by bus.

Chapter 7

Scotland

The Dows were real cockneys, who spoke in what's known as estuary English. In Kilmarnock the locals spoke with broad Scottish accents. Both sides struggled to make themselves understood. Despite this, everyone was friendly and welcoming. With the recent bombing of Glasgow, the people of Lugar certainly understood how important it was to help those who were victims of bombing campaigns 'doon sooth' as the Scots would say.

Joan thought she was making progress and beginning to feel at home when she made an error she never repeated. There'd been no warning that you should never walk on the outside of a pavement when passing a miner. Faces and arms blackened with the dirt of their previous shift, their lungs and throats would be filled with coaldust as they had no breathing apparatus to protect them underground. As they made their way home, they cleared whatever they could from their chests onto the roadway. Joan was so nearly the victim of a globule of gunk in her left ear, and learnt this lesson quickly. "Whoow!" Joan exclaimed as she dodged the flying gilbert to the cheers of the miners.

Joan in Nursing

She soon found out that many of the miners were affected by a severe disease called coal workers' pneumoconiosis, or 'black lung', plus another called silicosis. No wonder they tried to clear away the debris that congested their insides.

Hazel and Daphne found work in a nearby village, Hazel in a bakery, Daphne in a local grocery shop. The family had been sent to a cottage where Lil cooked all their meals on an open fire, with a stream nearby to do their washing and cleaning. Meanwhile, Joan was billeted to live with an elderly widow, Grace McKenna. It was from here that Joan walked to hospital every day to start her six months of nursing training.

At Grace's, the only heating was the coal fire Aga in the kitchen, and a log fire in the sitting room that covered everything and everywhere in dust. Not much warmth for a country so much colder than southern England, but Grace was frugal and concerned that any more would burn her money away.

Joan explained to Grace all about what had happened at home in Woodford. Grace in return told Joan about Glasgow being bombed earlier in the week.

"We need to put a stop to Mr Hitler," she said in her broad Scottish accent.

Immediately the two women were united in their common cause. Grace, with no children of her own, felt a sudden pride that Joan was about to train to be a nurse in her local area and do her bit for the war effort.

Grace was a kindly lady who had lost her husband in his late fifties. He'd been the pit manager in the local coal mine. She'd heard all about the Blitz, of course, and did her best to make her young visitor feel welcome, making her scones and

Dundee fruit cake which all the local children seemed to know about, and they'd tap on the window for their share.

One day Joan noticed that as Grace stood in the cold, stirring her baking mixture, a drip would sometimes fall slowly from her nose into the batter. Ugh. From then on, whenever she was offered the delicious baked goods, she would pretend to take a tiny nibble of the side and exclaim loudly how delicious it was, to cover her lack of appetite for the additional ingredient.

All in all, Ayrshire seemed pretty dull to Joan after all the excitement of London. The locals seemed rather inward-looking and she felt a bit out of place with her smart, shoulder-padded jackets and pencil skirts. As she left Grace's home to walk to the hospital, she hoped this was one part of her new life that she wouldn't regret.

A lot was expected of the new young nurses training at Kilbarchan Hospital in Kilmarnock, sometimes kept on their feet day and night taking care of patients as they learnt their craft. Being thrown in at the deep end in nursing was nothing like learning to be a bookkeeper in a stuffy classroom, thought Joan. On the other hand, the job had stopped Joan thinking about home, and in truth it suited her to a tee. Keeping patient notes and all the intricate detail involved in making sure all details were accurately listed reminded her of her skills developed working with lists of numbers at the Co-op.

She proudly dressed in her white uniform every shift. 'Absolutely no regrets,' she thought to herself every day, not even when she was cleaning up the worst of someone who was doubly incontinent with sickness to boot. Doing what she was doing, learning her new craft, somehow felt just right.

There was little light to work by at times in the hospital, and the nurses sometimes got by with the help of candles when the power went off. A cape for their shoulders and a welcome cup of cocoa was how they kept warm, together with a stove in the middle of the ward, the chimney going through the roof.

Joan's Nursing Badges

Joan's patients were local citizens with everyday illnesses and injuries. She often joked with them about the different accents they had to hers, helping to relax them and take their minds off any medical fears.

With pride she walked to and from work in her flared white skirt and tabard apron with a red cross on her sleeve and the hat worn by all nursing auxiliaries. She checked on pulse rates, blood pressure and when people had opened their bowels. She cleaned the floors, made the beds, emptied the bedpans, gave injections and fed the patients who couldn't feed themselves. All basic stuff, but a vital service for patients and doctors.

She was in Kilmarnock for just six months, the length of her training. It was a life of work, study, sleep and repeat. She grew proud of her new talents and with the way she built her relationships with those she cared for. It was meant to be.

It was now January 1944. It rained more in Scotland, there was thick snow in the winter, sometimes up to a foot deep. Local farmers with their tractors and snow ploughs cleared the roads so vehicles were able to run. Local business would clear their shop fronts, but the paths could be difficult to walk along with ice hidden under the snow to throw you off your feet.

Joan had passed all her nursing exams, both practical and theory. Her six months had passed quickly and she had forgotten about the discomforts and inconveniences as she scoured Matron's noticeboard for her next posting. Joan smiled to herself as she saw she had been posted to a newly adapted hospital in Bishop's Stortford, Hertfordshire, not so far from home. On the outskirts of London but in the countryside, it was far enough from the city to be free of bombing, she thought. Even better, the German war machine had begun to falter, and our troops had taken back North Africa and had started the invasion of Italy.

There were rumours of a second front, of the invasion of France. Britain had become a giant training ground with servicemen from across the globe. There was hope with the help of the US and Commonwealth that the tables were beginning to turn.

Joan thought about the speech that Churchill had made that she'd heard on the Light Programme on 10th November 1942, Churchill was speaking in the Guildhall at the Lord Mayor of London's banquet: "I have never promised anything but blood, toil, tears and sweat. Now, however, we have a new experience. We have a victory – a remarkable and definite VICTORY!"

Joan said her tearful farewells to her mum Lil, and to Hazel and Daphne, all still living in the cottage. She took a train back down south to Bishop's Stortford, to begin her next adventure, nursing those more directly affected by the war.

Chapter 8

Stansted

Bishop's Stortford Hospital was part old-style Victorian and part low lying, flat-rooved concrete, thirty miles northeast of central London. It was also just seven miles from the newly built aerodrome at Stansted Mountfitchet.

Joan thought the flat-roofed concrete structures, linked with their open-sided corridors looked pretty ugly. Their construction took less than a week, being just concrete sections on a concrete foundation. She found out about the reasons behind it early on during her time there.

The single-storey construction had been built so that if the hospital was bombed, some wards would still be serviceable. If the whole place had been several storeys high, the powers that be knew from experience that a single bombing might mean losing the whole building.

Joan crossed her fingers on both hands. "Blimey, being bombed once was more than enough," she muttered to herself.

Joan felt from the beginning that there was an eerie feel to the place – in part because of the bats that could land on your head at any moment as you wandered lost down the long corridors with their noisy, clanking pipework; in part because of the darkness that could fall at any time a blackout siren sounded. If Hitler had hoped to spook them, he had done a good job.

Stansted Mountfitchet Aerodrome, later known as Stansted, was built in 1942 by US engineers and used by the Strategic Royal Air Force and the United States Army Air Forces as a bomber airfield and maintenance depot. In 1943, when Joan started working as a nurse in Bishop's Stortford Hospital, Stansted became the base for the 344th Bombardment Group who'd arrived from Hunter Army Airfield in Georgia. Their motto: 'We win or die.' They had rather smart uniforms with the flying start motive on their upper arm.

Joan had been billeted in a room with another Essex girl, Elsie. They instantly felt at home with each other. Elsie shared her quarters. The two of them became as close as sisters.

"Thick as thieves, we are," Joan wrote back to her mum, who was still with the twins in Lugar.

Bert had been able to get an engineering job locally making shell cases. Joan felt warm inside to think they were back together as a family again.

Joan and Elsie weren't exactly built from the same stock. Joan was classically beautiful; she could click her fingers and men would come running. Elsie wasn't as good looking as Joan, but she certainly knew how to enjoy herself. To Joan's eyes she was a bit 'free with her favours', though she certainly didn't report that back to Lil.

"You should keep your hand on your farthing (London slang for the vagina)," Joan counselled her, while to Elsie, Joan should have 'loosened up a bit'.

"A girls gotta enjoy yourself, could be fried bread (dead) tomorra."

Beyond these differences, they knew how to support each other and themselves.

When Joan thought back to her early experiences in nursing in Kilmarnock, working on the general ward with those needing their appendix removed or their broken leg cared for, or with TB or a miner's lung disease, she realised she had no idea about what was to follow. It was a real shock to the system. Even the commanders arriving into her ward on stretchers, their lives devastated by their injuries, were often barely in their early twenties.

Walking into town, Joan saw the groups of smiling good-looking young US airmen waiting for the trucks to take them back to the base. She was saddened by the thought that so many would be lost.

Losses were harsh and numbers were high. A quarter of all of the lovely young men she saw queuing to climb into their trucks would end up MIA. All of those families would be left bereft. All of the women who'd paired up with them during their time over here faced devastation.

The aircraft would take off when the nurses were asleep, waking them suddenly as the rumble of the plane left the runways at midnight. They flew over Bishop's Stortford, on their way to Germany across the Channel. The noise of the engines joined together in a chorus that ran right through the bodies of those woken below. As the planes reached Germany when daylight hit, that's when they would drop their bombs and face the ack-ack anti-aircraft response from down below. The injuries they received were explosive ones as ack-ack shells exploded just before reaching their targets and destroyed everything in their reach. The shrapnel could make its way through the fuselage and reached the occupants inside.

Joan saw the impact of this when the men made it back to Blighty; shards of shrapnel dislodging a young man's eye, limbs being lost time and again, terrible injuries shocking air teams and nurses to the core. There were constant rows of stretchers being brought into their ward. Life after life lying in front of them, needing their help.

What, wondered Joan, had those fleets of young men thought as they were shipped over to the other side of the world. Would they have any idea of the future that greeted them? She admired them for their bravery, to the last man.

Joan learnt a lot about bombers. She'd overheard talk. The worst job, it seemed, was tail gunner. This was because the turrets that housed them were small and cramped. The planes were cruising at 10,000 feet where the temperature was often below freezing. The crew would be wearing fur- or fleece-lined boots and jackets but the tail gunners in their restricted turrets couldn't fit their parachutes on as well. There simply wasn't room. If something went wrong, they'd have to try to escape. The tail turret had to be rotated to allow for exit, with the hydraulics often failing at this stage, so the gunner would have to manually turn the turret. This took precious minutes before the gunner could escape and grapple with the straps of his parachute. Tail gunners often perished with their planes. The fuselage was full of pieces of metal so wasn't user-friendly for those inside. The more Joan learnt, the more grateful she was to all those fighting the fight she believed in so strongly.

The excitement she felt on her first day in her new role

never left her. She had chosen this path to do her bit for the war effort and she didn't regret that decision for a second. Not that everything suited her. The matron in Bishop's Stortford was much stricter, checking the uniforms of her charges as if they were new privates in an army regiment and telling them off for the slightest error. Joan had to concede at times that this pressure and these standards improved the way she worked and the level of care she took but the young nurses complained bitterly to each other at every telling-off.

"Frustrated old bitch," Elsie whispered under her breath.

Joan sniggered, "Don't" under her breath.

When they had time to themselves, the nurses developed their favourite ways to enjoy each other's company. Some had relations nearby and if one of the group had a car, they'd squeeze in together and drive off for a tea party, on occasion managing to lay their hands on a bottle of gin to cheer the afternoon away. Aunts would make wonderful cakes and sandwiches and create whatever else they could with their rations to reward the young nurses. All sorts of creativity was brought to bear to create anything that could resemble a cake as people remembered them, even though most were egg-less and almost fat free.

Back at work, sometimes their shifts would last day and night because an air raid would sound, and swarms of new patients would make their way to the wards. Or the servicemen would be carried in with the worst of what the Germans could do to them. It was tough.

The staff dealt with terrible injuries. Some pilots had been so badly burnt their own families wouldn't have recognised them. Shocking. Brutal. Some faced agonising days in intensive care before they died. The young nurses gave their all to help them deal with the indignities and tragedy of war.

One evening, to relieve themselves of the worst of what they'd witnessed that day, Joan and Elsie cadged a lift with an ambulance to the Nags Head pub in Much Hadham. Joan was good at chatting up the drivers. Joan had heard that the American officers used the Nags Head for R&R. It would be fun; Elsie was game too. The pair of them soon found themselves surrounded by handsome young men and were being treated to cocktails they hadn't heard of and yarns from back home.

Joan had a different way with men than Elsie. She knew how to get the best out of them and how to control them. She didn't let them get away with much. Arms' length was her rule. But it was here and now that she fell in love, against all her plans and expectations, with Frederick, an American pilot.

Frederick was the most handsome man she'd ever seen. He was tall and slim with blond, wavy hair. He seemed more mature than most. He was twenty-four and a Lieutenant who had worked his way up the ranks; a trained officer who became a trained pilot flying B-26 bombers, nicknamed Marauders. These were specially built for tactical bombing with an accurate bomb sight for pinpoint accuracy. They had a top speed of more than 300 mph and were a force to be reckoned with.

She first caught sight of him at the bar. He was tall, quite slim, with a moustache and looked dashing in his uniform. She soon found out he was both quiet and courteous, not like a lot of men who tipped their cap at her. Indeed, he and Joan were somewhat opposite. She was loud to his calm, cheeky to his gentleness. She was transfixed.

Her mind briefly flitted to the criticisms she'd had of Elsie and her other colleagues when she'd heard about their antics with some of the Americans they'd met. Maybe she had misjudged them. Maybe they too had met the kind of men they hadn't encountered before.

After an evening of talking, joking and laughing, Joan and Frederick moved outside, out of eyeshot of her friends and his, and kissed softly. She was really falling for him.

Joan knew Frederick would have a tour of a hundred missions, lasting two or three months. There was talk of an invasion of France, where his squadron was likely to be relocated.

"It's classified, Joan," he whispered.

"I wouldn't say a word," as she crossed her lips.

There would be a new batch of guys in B17 heavy bombers (nicknamed flying fortresses) who would take the place of him and those he was flying with.

In the back of her mind she knew this; she kept reminding herself that he wouldn't be here forever, even if he managed to keep himself safe from harm. The chances of that were miniscule.

Joan felt close to Frederick. She confided in her parents and her sisters about him, though she never told her husband when she married after the war. That secret was safely kept.

Joan and Frederick, who she called Freddie, met as often as they could.

One day Freddie told her, "We have one of the strongest planes. They can take so much damage and still fly home."

"Oh, I thought losses were high," said Joan.

USAAF Badge

"Well, sure," agreed Freddie. "It ain't a walk in the park but last week a Marauder came all the way back from a target over Belgium on one engine and landed in one piece with the undercarriage still up!"

"Oh my word!" Joan was shocked. "That sounds dangerous."

"Well yeah, but they had it flying again in a week."

'They're like flying tanks,' thought Joan.

"Freddie," Joan said, looking at Frederick eye to eye. "I don't want to be alarmed but that sounds really risky. What if it was your plane?" Her eyes were welling up.

Freddie paused. "I'm still here sweetie ..."

Joan drew a breath and slapped Frederick on the shoulder. "You mean it was you that crash-landed – the rear gunner had some nasty flack injuries, he was in my ward."

Freddie was smiling, holding his hand against his face to protect himself from any other blows that might come his way.

"Oh that was Jim Myers. That was bad luck – but he's OK now thanks to you guys."

Joan was shocked. She gently placed her arms around Freddie's neck. "I don't know what I'd do if I lost you," she told him softly. "I'm in love with you, Freddie."

"I love you too, sweetie," Freddie assured her. "Let's face it, I ain't been bombed like you."

"True, and you'd better stay safe, I need to know you're safe."

An idea suddenly hit Freddie. "Hey, we've got a refit coming up so I have some time to spare. Why don't we take a trip down to the coast? There's a nice hotel the guys were telling me about in Bog-nar Re-gus. Your king had a place there I hear."

Joan softened. "Oh I'm sorry I slapped you. I was so shocked," she told Freddie. "And it's pronounced Bognor Regis, the G is said like a J. Okey dokey I'll go there with you. But you had better stay safe then."

"Oh the English language is so complicated over here!"

Joan laughed. "Sure is," she smiled.

Joan managed to persuade Matron to give her two days off work.

Back in their room, Elsie remarked, "Lucky you to get a dirty weekend with a yank."

"Stop it," Joan retorted. "Freddie's not like that."

344th Bombardment Group We win or Die

Elsie laughed. "Overpaid, over here and oversexed," she uttered under her breath while pulling on a new pair of stockings.

"Where did you get those?" asked Joan.

"Just a gift from an admirer," said Elsie with a wink.

"I bet," replied Joan, and they both roared with laughter.

The Bognor weekend started well. Freddie managed to get a friend to drive them to the Bishop's Stortford station. Crossing London took time and by the time they arrived in

Bognor it was nearly 9pm. They found the place they were staying. Burlington Hotel was magnificent, a Victorian building with gold-leaf lettering on the sign which stretched the length of the facade.

Joan thought it looked luxurious. The blacked-out windows made it look like it was closed, but once inside it was splendid. Polished wooden floors and comfy leather Chesterfield armchairs.

'I could get used to this,' thought Joan.

Freddie had booked a sea-view room overlooking the pier. A couple of gins later, Joan had fallen asleep in the high-backed armchair by the window. Freddie gazed at her face. She looked really relaxed and beautiful by the light of the moon through the window. He carefully took her shoes off and laid her on the bed, pulling the floral eiderdown over her. He had never been more at home with someone.

The next day started with a bright, sunny morning with fluffy white puffs of cloud and an onshore breeze. Joan woke and found herself fully dressed, wondering where the seductive evening had gone. Freddie was sleeping next to her in his underwear, he looked relaxed and peaceful. It seemed they'd come all this way to get a peaceful night's sleep, without the droning squadrons of bombers taking off at the early hours in the morning disturbing them. It was so peaceful, just the sound of seagulls, and the tumbling tide displacing the pebbles along the shore.

How romantic, thought Joan. Were they still in the same world, she wondered.

After a good breakfast and a kiss to equal any she'd seen in the movies, they walked along the seafront to the pier.

"Freddie, this is lovely. I'd forgotten how a good night's sleep feels," she told him.

"Yep, me too," he agreed.

Freddie and Joan managed to meet up sometimes at her billet. Though it was frowned upon; the notice on the door was 'females only'. Like many others, Joan sneaked Freddie in when Elsie was on shift. Joan held Freddie's hand with a finger to her lips. "Shush!" she uttered under her breath.

Freddie smiled, whispering, "Sure, there is a war on you know."

"Stop it!" Joan retorted, tip-toeing into the passageway.

Chapter 9

Two endings

At the end of her shift, Joan began to worry. She hadn't heard from Freddie for several days and decided to do her best to seek him out.

Phil, one of the hospital porters with a motorcycle, offered to run her up to the barracks. Joan looked around her as he drove. There were military trucks everywhere. She didn't know if she'd ever seen things so busy. Military Police with whistles were waving their arms, directing the vehicles this way and that.

Joan dismounted. "Thanks, Phil," she told her colleague.

"Do you want me to wait?" he asked her.

Joan thanked him but said, "It's OK, I'll get a lift. I'll spot someone I know."

She knew her nurses' uniform was visible under her coat. While public transport was scarce, most service personnel felt obliged to give lifts, especially to nurses because of the important work they did.

Their hospital was known to them all – there wasn't anyone who hadn't been there either as a visitor or a patient. Joan entered the red-brick guardroom as Phil's motorcycle spluttered on the low-grade fuel as it accelerated away.

A US Airforce Military Policeman with his smart red-banded cap was on duty behind the wooden desk.

"Can I help you, young lady?" he asked.

"Yes," she replied. "I was hoping to talk to Lieutenant Frederick Peterson."

"Sorry I don't think that's possible – we're all on a high alert."

Joan suddenly made sense of the activity she'd seen all around her.

"Is this the D-Day invasion?" she asked.

"I can't say. The camp is locked down," came the reply.

Joan turned away in time to see a group of B-26s taking off on the runway. Was one of these Freddie's plane?

"You can write a note. I'll make sure he gets it," she was reassured.

Joan took an old envelope from her bag, crossing out the address on the front and writing *Lt Frederick Peterson* on the front. She wrote on the back, *I was so worried, hadn't heard from you for days, hope you're safe and well … Love Joan.* Folding the envelope, she handed it to the corporal slightly embarrassed by the content, hoping he wouldn't read it.

"I'll see he gets it," the corporal uttered, putting the envelope into a box marked 'In Mail'.

Joan smiled and turned, making for the door.

There seemed to be a constant line of vehicles of all types driving past the gate. Joan spotted an ambulance and waved them down.

"Bishops Stortford 'ospital!" he shouted with a broad grin.

Joan recognised the driver Steve; the nurses got to know all the drivers. She hopped in.

"Thanks Steve!" she said as she squeezed past Margaret, the attendant, and sat between them.

"Lucky you saw us, it's about to rain." He could see Joan looked tearful.

Two days later, on 6th June, Joan received a postcard from Freddie.

Sorry sweetie, it read, *We're on flying missions back-to-back, I'll let you know when I get a break. love Frederick.*"

It was nearly the end of June when Freddie finally turned up at Joan's ward.

"Hi," he said, his smile reaching from one side of his face to the other.

"Freddie," Joan smiled back in shock and delight. She placed a syringe she'd been holding into a bowl and ran towards him.

"Is your matron around?" wondered Freddie, not wanting to get Joan one of her regular tellings-off.

"Well I guess not!" Joan replied, grabbing his hand and drawing the curtains round an empty bed.

One of the patients opposite spotted them and gestured to the man in the bed beside him.

Joan and Freddie embraced and kissed. It was like a black cloud had lifted. Joan felt as if she was back on the seafront at Bognor. Then reality struck. "Can't let Matron catch us like this. I'll never hear the end of it."

"Sure, I'll pick you up when you're off. Chris has lent me his car for the evening."

They hugged and kissed again. Joan led Freddie out of the ward in time to see Matron walking down towards them. Joan composed herself.

"Sorry, Lieutenant, your colleague doesn't seem to be in this ward."

Freddie turned to see the expression on Matron's face. "Sure, I'll be on my way."

"Can I help you, young man?" asked Matron, suspiciously.

"The Lieutenant got the wrong ward, Matron," Joan responded.

"You'd better straighten your apron, Nurse Dow. We don't want the Lieutenant to think we are slapdash." There was a slight smile at the edges of her lips.

"Okey dok … err yes Matron," replied Joan, slightly flustered.

When they met later, Freddie gave Joan the news that his squadron was being transferred to an aerodrome at the Advanced Landing Ground at Cormeilles-en-Vexin, in France.

"When will I see you again?" she asked him.

"I guess when we've won." Freddie grinned. "I guess there'll be a new squadron of liberators to keep you all entertained."

"Stop it, you know I'll wait for you Freddie, I love you more than anything," Joan scolded him.

"I know, sweetie. You know I feel the same."

The first operation saw thirty-seven crews taking part in bombings in Normandy and the D-Day landings. Germany was bombed too. Joan was one of hundreds of thousands of personnel in place to back these forces. There were one hundred and forty-six US missions in seven months, with twenty-six aircraft lost.

When crew went missing or were killed, the barracks

would post an MIA list – Missing In Action. Joan regularly scanned the lists hoping not to see Freddie's name. Relief flooded her every cell each time she looked.

All seemed well until one day she spotted Frederick's friend Sam in the Nags Head. He looked sad, deep in thought. She went over to him and he confirmed the worst.

"Emm ah," he stuttered. "Freddie's plane was MIA. There has been no word."

Sam stood there in deep thought. "Joan, don't fret. This happens all the time. He may have crash-landed; he may have been captured. I know Freddie would do everything to get back to you. These things are never a foregone conclusion. It's crazy out there."

Crash Landings

Joan didn't know the scream that left her body was hers. She genuinely thought it belonged to someone else. Familiar arms embraced her. "Frederick?" she guessed, but no. This was her friend Elsie, whose kindness gave her tears permission to flow. Elsie led Joan back home to the nurses' quarters to cry out her tears alone in isolated dignity.

When Freddie went missing, a part of Joan went missing too. He had filled her heart, and she was bereft without him. She did her best to focus at work, her mind drifting just once. She was working in the middle of a blackout, scarcely able to see, when a patient called out to her. Startled, she turned and fell onto an oil heater in the ward that had been left with no safety guard, and burnt her arm severely, spending some several weeks in Haymeads Hospital's burns unit as an inpatient.

Once sufficiently healed, still with the dressing on, Joan persuaded the doctors to let her go back to her duties at Bishop's Stortford.

As the weeks and months passed, she realised Frederick had taught her a powerful lesson. She now knew what it meant to love and accept someone else without judgement. She may have been wrung out and left to dry on the washing line of life, but it had taught her something valuable: that she was capable of deep love. A lesson she had secretly yearned to learn.

Work presented her with some distraction. She'd nursed some German pilots who'd been shot down over England as they'd done their darndest to destroy the cities and factories and transport hubs over here. One, she noted, was a 'real Nazi'. They all hated him. He told them constantly they were useless, and that Hitler was right and would win the war. They did all they could to silence him, using a needle specially blunted whenever he needed an injection.

"Serves him right. Ron and Freddie would be proud," she

said to herself.

But then, while Joan was still in shock from Freddie's disappearance, along came Hans. Yes, he was German, but he was truly a lovely man and in desperate need of hospital care. He had parachuted from his Heinkel bomber and had extensive burns as well as a broken leg. She could see he was terribly weak. In desperate pain and a long way from home, he confided in Joan.

"I never wanted to fight this war," he told her. "I'm embarrassed to be here. I don't believe anything my country is doing is right. I hate that Nazi bastard," he explained. "He calls me a traitor. That's why they moved my bed."

Joan understood the torment this airman had; she felt sympathy towards him.

Joan spoke gently back to him. "How can you speak such good English?" she asked.

He told her about his time in England before the war. "I study at Oxford University, economics." Hans paused, with anguish in his voice. "I have many friends there."

Joan thought about how Freddie could be facing the same fate. She imagined him being injured and a German nurse caring for him. She was determined to do her best to help Hans recover; she felt it her duty.

Joan shared what Hans had told her with the other nurses. She wanted everyone to be kind to him. Unlike the others, these words hadn't surprised her. She had strong memories of her German penfriend, Eva, from before the war. She knew the Germans were ordinary people, many of them brainwashed but many of them victims too. She wondered with deep concern what had happened to Eva's family. She knew Munich had been heavily bombed by the Allies. She hoped her family had survived. She knew pain and fear could be experienced by both sides. Although she hated Hitler and the Nazi regime, these young men had families back home who faced the anguish she did, and they were brought into the conflict like everyone else and asked to take sides. Thanks to Hans, Joan learnt very quickly what it was like to live a life without judgement. She never knew if she was going to be alive that evening, the next day or the next week. She knew she just had to live her life and that's exactly what she did.

The war years was the most exciting time of her life. She took every day as it came, living for the present. There was no point getting depressed about anything. If you died, you'd be dead anyway and nobody would know if you'd been depressed or not. Cigarettes and alcohol took the edge off everyone's feelings, together with copious amounts of the sweetest tea, that often tasted sugared to the brim.

There was a lot of not knowing. As she nursed Hans, she thought of Freddie. She thought of his smile and his laugh, of the tricks he played on her, hiding her drinks, teasing her. She thought of the way she called him 'a sod', something he'd never heard before and he echoed that back to her in his fake London accent. She had no idea where he was. Alive, dead, in prison, lost and stranded, even being sheltered by kind people. No one knew the answer.

Then she thought of Hans and realised the same was true of his family. They would be thinking, where is he? What happened to him? They wouldn't know. True enough, the Red Cross used to come around and take names, and then pass information over to the Germans and the Germans were passing information back, but how long would that take? Probably months. Some of the information would undoubtedly be held back. Military secrets and all.

One day she walked into work as happy as she always was. She no longer thought about Freddie every day, though she knew she could never forget him. She opened the door into her ward, waiting to greet her colleagues and avoid the most frightening aspects of Matron's critical eye.

Suddenly her blood ran cold. The bed where Hans had lain was empty. Nothing there. Another nurse, someone she hadn't seen before, was efficiently shaking out a clean white sheet and crisply covering the mattress, ready for a new patient. Elsie rushed to her side.

"He's gone," she whispered. "He didn't make it."

Elsie desperately tried to make things better. She knew how much loss her friend had already lived through.

"It's probably for the best …" she tried to say. "He was in such pain …"

None of this should have surprised Joan. Eighty per cent burns was almost impossible to survive, if she had given any time to think things through. Yet, after Frederick, Hans had been the first man who had touched her heart. He'd truly meant something to her. She understood him. She believed in him. And he trusted her – a nurse from across enemy lines. They had a shared humanity.

Silent tears ran down her face. Elsie held her tight. They all knew this feeling.

****

Joan did all she could to put difficult feelings behind her. She would still go to the pub. She'd play the piano and sing songs – Vera Lynn's 'We'll Meet Again' was a regular request. How Bert would have loved to have seen her entertaining everyone in this way. As she played for her friends, she knew the song wasn't always true. Not everyone would see those they loved again.

She made a decision and she kept to it. Never again during the war would she fall for someone. She couldn't bear the loss. Enough was truly enough.

Until the end of the war, Joan continued to love nursing. So much was familiar to someone who had been such an efficient bookkeeper. She thought back to her colleagues at the Co-op and wondered if her life now would surprise them.

She loved immersing herself in the facts and figures of life. Just as you had to count the pennies at the local shop, you had to make sure your patient notes in the hospital were just so. Accuracy was so important. Everything from monitoring blood pressure and its ups and downs to doing the same with your patients' temperature and heartbeat. The rules were the same – keeping everything up to date, keeping everything legible and in order. People think nursing is about kindness, and it is, but it's also about facts and figures. It suited her down to the ground. She felt this in Kilmarnock and realised it even more strongly in Bishop's Stortford.

Of course, no one at the Co-op would have treated her in the way Matron did. They were much more of a team there. And the doctors treated them all as servants, even asking them to fetch them cups of tea, but none of this mattered when Joan thought about how important her work was in the grand scheme of things. This was what the country needed.

Her pay had risen from £62 and 10s a year at the beginning to £95 just after the end of the war. It was then she was awarded her SRN – Senior Registered Nurse – pin. One word on her report stood out loud and proud. Her work, the examiner said, had been 'exemplary'. She wondered if, after all the tellings-off and scoldings, it had been Matron who had provided that feedback.

For six long years, first with her family, then with her fellow nurses, she gathered with people she loved round the radio, avidly, ardently listening for good news. It was only once the Allies invaded France and pushed the Germans back that there was true cause for hope. Then on VE Day came true relief. The triumph. Joan, Grace and their friends were given the night off. They took the train to Liverpool Street Station and the bus into town and went and celebrated like everyone else, out to Trafalgar Square to join the party.

A few weeks before VE day, an ambulance driver had pulled up outside her hospital. It was a young woman, very well spoken, Joan remembered. Joan approved. Everyone was playing their part, she knew, even people from the poshest parts of London.

In the ambulance was a wounded soldier, not wounded in battle but in a road accident in the town, leaving him with a broken arm and shoulder, and covered in bruises.

Joan looked at the driver, who was called Libby. She looked familiar. Joan wondered if she knew her from somewhere but couldn't place her. This wasn't a surprise. She knew so many people from all her different experiences. Before she could say anything, the co-driver said, "All right, Libby, let's go," and they drove away.

Years and years later Joan realised where she 'knew' Libby from. This was HM Queen Elizabeth II – at the time HRH Princess Elizabeth – playing her own part in the war effort.

The war was now drawing to a close. Many soldiers had lived through the atrocities of battle, the fear and the pain and the death. Joan, too, had seen and lived through more than most people realised. She had a deep knowledge and deep understanding of war from both sides. She breathed a long and deep sigh of relief. It was over.

Chapter 10

Search for normality

Few can have been as busy after the war as those in the building trade. Everywhere was rubble where buildings should have been. Everywhere were gaps in rows of houses where some unlucky blighters lost their home. There was work to be done.

In time, Waverley Road was repaired. The front of the Dow's home was reglazed, the roof damage was sorted, and new homes were erected opposite theirs. Mum, Hazel and Daphne came back down from Lugar, Bert from his lodgings, Ron from overseas, and Joan from her nursing quarters. Back they went to their old lives, Joan even returning to life at the Co-op.

Rationing continued, of course, and life was hard for many as they gathered up their harshest experiences and the grief they felt and hid it deep inside themselves, placing making a living and making ends meet at the forefront of their days.

The National Health Service was set up. 'Thank goodness,' thought Joan. She knew so much now about the significance of good medical care.

Bert was thrilled to have his family back home together. He was something of an artist and started painting with oils, creating beautiful pictures and patterns on the panels of the wooden inside doors.

Tragically, the Dean family, who bought the house from Bert and Lil, decided to cover the panels over with boarding. Plain and simple flush doors were now of the moment, apparently. Innovation is not always for the best.

****

On the day of her return, Joan stood outside 49 Waverley Road and thought about their old lives. The war in the Pacific was still raging. Ron had mentioned he may be sent to the Pacific, possibly to help with the stores and supplies to aid the Allied troops in taking back Malaya.

Joan could feel her eyes welling up again. Not for the first or last time she was thinking of Freddie. In that very moment Hazel opened the front door.

"Joan!" she yelled. "Come in. We 'ave a visitor from France."

Joan found a smile and said, "'Oos that?"

"Monica."

"Monica?" Joan repeated, realising who Monica was.

She recalled the story that Ron had told her when he met her in Bishop's Stortford a few weeks after the terrible news about Freddie.

Bless Ron. He'd been transferred back to Paris after France was liberated from North Africa and had taken leave when he'd heard about Freddie. It had taken a day to get a ship back across the Channel. In those days there was a constant steam of supply vessels going back and forth.

He turned up at Joan's ward looking so smart in his army battledress with his two stripes and beret folded neatly under his lapel. He'd been such a comfort.

Christmas from Freddie

Ron said he'd met a beautiful French girl in Paris called Monica and they planned to marry.

"Where's Ron?" Joan asked putting her suitcase down in the hallway.

"Oh!" Hazel exclaimed with surprise. "You don't know? They broke up." She paused to take a breath and added in a low whisper, "Monica is in the garden with Daphne and Mum."

Their mum and dad had first met Monica in France when they went over to discuss the wedding plans with Monica's parents. It had sounded like a great trip and full steam ahead for the happy day.

Hazel explained that things hadn't quite worked out. "You know how Ron is a supporter of Socialism?"

"Go on," urged Joan.

"Well Ron doesn't believe in religion but Monica's a Catholic. Her parents were insisting Ron became a Catholic."

"Oh," Joan sighed. "'E wouldn't 'ave that."

"No – and Monica is so sweet she's come all this way to apologise and make up."

It was all too late. Ron had since met Betty, his wife-to-be.

They went into the garden to meet their guest. Monica was charming, very pretty and petite, with long brown wavy hair. It was a surprise to hear that Ron had broken up with such a lovely creature. Her English was quite good and she had a very sexy French accent like Marlene Dietrich.

She'd brought a bottle of French Beaujolais red wine and they sipped together, discussing their wartime experiences. Monica spoke of the hardship under Nazi occupation, how some girls had gone out with German soldiers.

"When Paris was liberated with the US and British forces, there was much celebration," she told them in her beautiful accent. "But these girls were made spectacles of, partisans stripping their dresses and shaving their heads."

Monica talked about how strict her parents were, wanting her to marry a Catholic and Joan thought how lucky she was to have freedom, despite everything she had been through. She thought of all those lovely young American airmen who never returned home. She also knew that Germans like Hans were just another tragedy of the war.

Every day she counted her blessings. Everyone who had survived and whose families were intact. Peacetime brought with it a yearning to build a normal life, to marry and have children and that's just what Joan did.

She met Reggie Young, the son of another Reginald. He was from Barnet, a middle-class family, as Reg senior was an accountant for a London stockbroker. This was another world. He went to his office in a suit and bowler hat. His mum was Maud who was a bit of a snob. She'd come from the Moody family who owned a marine engine business in Rotherhithe.

Reggie had a younger sister Sylvia who had trained in tap dance and had appeared in many amateur shows.

Reg was thirty-one at the end of war. He was taller than average, had a slim build with a rather dashing moustache. Joan had met Reg briefly before the war when he came to the house with Stan, one of her distant cousins.

After the war, one Sunday afternoon Reg turned up on his Panther 600cc motorcycle to see Ron who was also into bikes. Joan was in the sitting room playing some sheet music of a Glen Miller number, a favourite from Much Hadham. She stopped playing when she heard the thump, thump at the door. It had rained earlier, and Reg was a bit wet even though he had his old army trench coat on. The droplets of water dribbled off his curly hair.

"Could have done with a hat," Ron told him.

"Bloody thing blew off," said Reg, removing his goggles.

Joan stepped out from behind Ron. "You look wet. Come in and warm up," she told him.

Joan thought how handsome and sexy he looked. In fact, he reminded her of Freddie.

"'Ave you come far, Reg?" asked Joan.

"From Barnet," he told her. "I managed to get some black-market fuel for the bike – it's been in storage during the war."

Now there was a great deal to catch up on. Reg had married in the war. His wife had given birth to a baby who had died and had then disappeared from Reg's life. He sobbed as he recounted the story to Joan.

Joan agreed to take a spin on pillion with Reg, and she snuggled up to Reg's back with her arms around his waist.

"You won't go too fast, will you?"

Reg smiled, "Not if I want to get home on this tankful."

Their relationship soon flourished.

Joan went out on Reg's Panther many times, even as far as Devon. She used to admit that she'd sometimes fall asleep as she held on to him as Reg was a confident and smooth rider.

Joan felt sure she could build the life with Reg that she wanted. She soon found out the match nearly didn't happen. It was the Nazis who could have put a stop to it. Reg was working on radar during the war when a doodlebug landed on the unit where he was working. As it happened, he had chosen that very moment to walk to the NAAFI to get a cup of tea. As he crossed the field he heard the doodlebug's droning engine stop, and a whistle as it nosedived to the ground.

With that, Reg dived for the ground too. "It felt like the ground came up to hit me!"

The radar unit was in the centre of the field with the ack-ack units distributed around like a spoked wheel. The doodlebug made a direct hit on Reg's radar set. It was fortunate for Reg that he left his radar unit when he did, otherwise it would have been certain death. The ack-ack units around the perimeter were also unscathed.

In Reg's words, "I was bloody lucky."

Their wedding was in 1948 at the Methodist Church on George Lane and the reception at the Majestic Cinema, like most couples of the time where they lived. Then they went on honeymoon by steam train to Dartmouth in Devon where they stayed with a landlady called Mrs Pinny in her guesthouse.

They loved Mrs Pinny and returned to see her in the years that followed.

Among all her possible suitors, Joan had felt satisfied to set her stall on Reg. An electrical engineer, he was the opposite to her. She was gregarious, he was quiet, though they both had a temper. Joan persuaded Reg to buy one of the rebuilt homes opposite her parents. There was a serious shortage of property after the war and when her sister Hazel and her husband Roy Ellis were married, they rented the front bedroom to them.

Roy was younger so he was spared the European conflict; he'd trained for the Japanese conflict. However, the first H bomb put an end to that, and he ended his national service in India. This was a harrowing experience as Partition was in full flow and there were the most awful atrocities taking place between the Hindus and Muslims.

Reg being a qualified electrician, installed a cooker point so that Roy and Hazel had the privacy of a bedsit.

Reg was a clever and practical man. He understood intricate details about how things worked. He worked for ITT in Potters Bar and then with Plessy in Ilford where he designed circuitry for military and domestic radar and communications systems. Most radar installations in the UK today will have circuitry designed by Reg Young.

In 1973, Plessey got the contract for a new multi-channel UHF portable communication pack called the MANPACK. Reg was the chief draftsman at the time.

"The Department of Defence wrote a spec that's almost impossible to manufacture. It's got to operate in -20 degrees and plus-50 degrees and survive being run over by a tank!" he exclaimed in disbelief.

Joan tended to dominate the marriage. She had a strong mind and strong principles and stuck to them. Reg had his pride and his strong intelligence. At times, Joan felt frustrated with real life. The war had taken away six long years. They wanted normality to return. Everyone wanted that.

And you do sometimes get what you want. In 1949 on November 5th in the late evening in Wanstead Hospital, with fireworks blasting into the peacetime Guy Fawkes night sky, Joan gave birth to a little baby boy, her first son, Paul.